Three Maestros

Three Maestros

Dr. Pratibha Ray

Translated by
Sankar Narayan Mallick

BLACK EAGLE BOOKS
Dublin, USA
Bhubaneswar, India

BLACK EAGLE BOOKS

USA address:
7464 Wisdom Lane
Dublin, OH 43016

India address:
E/312, Trident Galaxy, Kalinga Nagar,
Bhubaneswar-751003, Odisha, India

E-mail: info@blackeaglebooks.org
Website: www.blackeaglebooks.org

First International Edition Published by
BLACK EAGLE BOOKS, 2024

THREE MAESTROS
A novellet for children by **Pratibha Ray**

Translated by **Sankar Narayan Mallick**

Cover & Interior Design: Ezy's Publication

ISBN- 978-1-64560-611-6

Printed in the United States of America

This tale has its origin in telling stories
to the three Ustads of my world.
This book is dedicated to them,
Adyasha (Dozy), **Anwesh** (Rocky),
Ayaskant (Lucky)
and all the mini-Maestros
of every household.

- **Writer**

CONTENTS

A Picnic in the Offing

They were three in number; Oltu, Paltu and Dholki. Oltu and Paltu were two brothers in that order and Dholki was the youngest one, their sister. All the three outsmarted one another. They were neither stupid nor bad. But the boys were up to a bit of mischief always, restless to the core. All round the clock, as if their hands, legs, and limbs were all eager to move. Dholki of the unkempt hair was not naughty as such, but if she sulked, she became immobile, like an anthill. Neither would she eat, nor would she open a book. Oltu and Paltu, too, when upset with the parents, let loose their anger on studies. At the drop of a hat, there was a threat from all three, "If it so happens, then we shall not study. Give me this, give me that; else I will not go to school today."

Day in and day out, parents were busy in persuading them, "Dear ones! Do not speak evil, don't look at evil and don't listen to evil. Heed the words of the Father of the Nation." They urged upon them to be obedient, not to ignore studies, not to waste time, not to put off till tomorrow what could be done today. "Wealth, once lost, could be recovered, but time and tide waits for none. Study when you should study and play when you should play." Parents had put the picture of Mahatma Gandhi and the statues of the three monkeys in the rooms of all the three with a wish that they would grow up to be good human beings.

Like medicine, which is at times bitter, this advice was not agreeable to the three siblings. They thought, "These parents are very obstinate. They are in the habit of telling always, 'Don't do this and don't do that.' It is fun to do whatever one likes. What is there to think so much in matters of fun and delight?"

The Annual Exams were knocking at the door. But all the three kids now insisted to go for a picnic.

This was the height of their whims. How

would the parents agree to it? They reasoned, "Let the exams be over. We can have the picnic afterwards, and your enjoyment, to the hilt." But the children were bent upon it. The wise words of their parents were ignored. The three kids hit upon the idea of running away to the jungle at the end of the neighbouring village in the wee hours of morning the next Sunday. They could take with them food materials like rice, dal and the like. Of course, a great feast in the forest would follow. They would get up on the trees, bathe in the wild fountains, fly in the air, befriend the butterflies, deer and doves, and threaten the wild animals like tigers and bears. They would eat fruits, deck flowers on themselves and sing songs! If the parents would ask later, they would say innocently, twinkling their eyes, "We had gone to the teachers to get guidance. We had been there all day long, forgetting food and drinks, immersed in studies. Now it has all ended and we are back home!" Parents would surely have a good word for them. Oltu and Paltu clapped and burst into laughter. Dholki pulled a long face: "No, I shall not go with you. Bunking studies and lying to elders would be a loss to ourselves. We shall pay for it when we get plucked in the exams…", said Dholki.

Oltu got annoyed hearing her answer "Don't come then, no one flatters you to do so. Keep studying at home. We shall have fun in the forest. Do you think we shall bring back some fun in our pocket for you, like ground nuts from the market?

Paltu joined, "God only knows what you shall read at home. Your eyes shall be on the book and mind will be in the wild. You shall have neither study nor fun. You will be crying and rueing after we leave."

Paltu may be the younger one but had the gift of the gab. He could move someone to do the impossible by his words. Dholki was hardly able to control herself after hearing him. She too got ready. All three decided they will be heading out before dawn.

Dholki was apprehensive. "How shall we go in the dark? Shall we not feel afraid?"

Fourteen-year-old Oltu bragged, "What fear? I am with you. Who are you afraid of?"

Paltu said, "Fie on you! Being my sister, such fear in you! India is the land of heroes. Baji Rout, hardly twelve years old, sacrificed his life for the country with a smile on his face. Dharmapada, another twelve-year-old jumped into the sea to save twelve hundred craftsmen and immortalised his name. The brave girls of this country like Laxmibai of Jhansi and Queen Durgavati became martyrs fighting the enemy and defending the country. How can you be so afraid?"

Dholki assured them, "No, no I am not a bit afraid. I just told you so. I am also with you. I am game for going out on our Picnic."

Three Siblings Set Out

Three siblings set out before dawn, leaving their warm beds, inebriate with the wish for a picnic. They packed some rice, dal, and vegetable along with books and notes in the school bags. They also took some medicines, Dettol, Neosporin, Volini for pain and sprain, gauze cotton, bandage cloth, small pair of scissors and Vicks tablet for cold. It would all come in handy.

The three children were walking with their bags slung over their shoulders. No one would suspect them of moving into the forests. People would rather think them to be too good, setting out to study before the break of dawn. The three were walking with smiles on their faces. They had told the old housekeeper at home to tell mother that they were going to the teachers for studies, and she should not worry or look for them. They were serious for the exams and would return in the evening.

It was noon when they reached the jungle. Their legs were tired, and they were hungry by then. They arranged stones to work like a chullah and collected dry wood. They had rice and dal, but nothing as a container. How would they cook now? They had not thought about these issues. Worried and seeking, they looked here and there. A piece of broken pot was lying by the river. Someone had abandoned it. They gleefully brought that big shard of a pot and used it as a pan to cook rice, dal, and vegetables on it. There was no knife to slice the vegetables, but everything was still mixed and well-cooked. They fetched a banana leaf, cleaned it. They were all agog that they had been able to cook khichdi. It was without salt, but everything is delicious when one is hungry. Moreover, it was they themselves who had cooked it all. It was like nectar to them. They were feeling the sweet joy of working together to make food for the first time. Hardly had they started to eat when a tiny dog came out of a bush nearby. It looked hungry and had an entreating look in the eyes. It might have been starving for days.

They took the dog close and noticed that the mother was lying dead in the bushes. All started to feed the orphan dog with care. They let themselves remain ill-fed to let the tiny baby eat well. It was mute so it could not speak and ask. "But being human we have to take care of her," they thought.

Eating was over. The wind was cool and soothing. It was telling them, as it were, to sleep for some time, to be rejuvenated. Without a sound they were asleep. When they got up, it was all dark and cicadas were singing in the forest. There was no light with them. How to get back home? But they were not afraid. The more nervous one becomes, the more danger tightens its grip. And it becomes difficult to wriggle out of it. Oltu, barely fourteen, assumed the tone of a forty-year-old and said, "Day and night is the same in the jungle. Our house has not shifted afar just because it is night. We shall go back moving step by step. Come, follow me. Dholki, are you afraid?"

Dholki held his hands tight and said, "Why should I be afraid? God is with us. When I have two brothers like Kalia and Balia* with me, why should I care?"

Twelve-year-old Paltu thumped his chest and boasted, "It is all less than enough for me. Brother need not be bothered about this. Let him lead the way. You walk in the middle. I am at the back and keeping a watch."

Ten-year-old Dholki was in the middle and they continued their walk back home. Dholki was humming a bhajan in her sweet tone to break the monotony of the journey. As if the flora and fauna were attentive to her singing. Brothers were also at peace. No thorn was touching them, as it were. As if a road was opening before them by

---

Kalia and Balia refer to Jagannath and Balabhadra, two brothers of Devi Subhadra.

grace divine. as if someone was leading Oltu invisibly. A black animal was leading the way silently ahead of them. God-sent, as it were. Otherwise, how would they proceed so smoothly in the dark in a jungle!

They did not know how far they had traversed. They saw both the night and the road were nearing an end. The stretch of forest was about to be over. There was the light of dawn in the eastern sky. They would reach home soon. Someone was leading the way, walking ahead. Oh! it was that tiny puppy! Then he had led them safely through jungle track fraught with dangers of holes, thorns, pitfalls, and the like. How faithful was the animal! It had tried to repay the debt of the feeding and the rescue! Could such a friend be forsaken? They would take him home. They should nourish him. For such a bold and helpful role, he would be named Bahadur.

■

In An Unknown City

Forest ended here and the city began. No worry now. They could lead the way. Bahadur was now their guest.

But what was this? They were now in a new town! They had travelled in the dark in the opposite direction and were now quite far off. What to do now? They became upset with

Bahadur. He had led them on this route, and all this was now because of him. But after some time, they came to know that a tiger had come out and created a menace, killing cattle and buffalos. The road on the other side had been closed for safety. They became thankful to Bahadur yet again. He had, in fact, saved their lives. They would have been a delicious meal for the ferocious animal otherwise. They were sorry and ashamed for having blamed him. If one blames others without trying to understand, friends become foes. It was a lesson. They felt like being more discreet and considerate now.

The new town was looking nice. They thought they would travel a bit and explore it. If they return with new experience from a new place, parents too would be happy.

They were walking and Bahadur was ahead of them. They were tired and hungry. Still, they had the wish to see the whole of the city. Oltu asked a gentleman about the worth-seeing places in that city. As they were new to the city, they would see it all and get back to their town by the evening. The gentleman was quite happy at his gentle behaviour and smooth talk.

He gave an overall idea about the places worth visiting in that city. But it would be quite tedious taking a walk all over the city. So, they got onto a bus without thinking much. Bahadur followed suit. The dog slept below the conductor's seat. Once the bus started off, Oltu realized it was a mistake of theirs, as there was no money with them to book the tickets. Travelling without tickets is a mistake. It is a loss not to a person only, but to the country too. He said to the conductor in a sad tone, "Sir, if you please stop the bus here, we three shall get down."

Hearing his sweet words, the conductor told affectionately, "Why should you get down in this desolate place, there is hardly any house in sight here. I shall let you get down near your home."

Paltu folded his hands, "Sir, it is our mistake. We do not have money. We do not want to be ticketless travellers. So, if you let us get down here, we shall walk home. We forgot about the ticket while getting into the bus. Always we go with our father. We are never in the habit of booking tickets for ourselves."

The conductor was surprised at their gentle

behaviour and honesty. Nowadays, students stop the buses and get onto it in any place as per their sweet will. They create issues too to book the proper ticket. Sometimes they threaten the conductor. If forced to get down, they create a scene or scuffle quite often. So, when he saw students, he stopped the bus and took them along to avoid troubles. Many have taken for granted the right of students moving in the bus without tickets. So, the behaviour of these three children surprised him. Dholki was way too afraid after realizing that they had boarded the bus without a ticket. Her eyes were wet with tears. The conductor cafunéed her unkempt hair and asked with affection, "You too have not booked a ticket?" There were two drops of tears dropping like pearls from the eyes of Dholki. She told in a tremulous voice, "We shall never do this mistake again. We shall board a bus only after booking a ticket."

The conductor told in a soothing voice, "Nothing to worry now! I am booking three tickets for all of you for your good behaviour and truthfulness. If this honesty of yours has an influence on your friends, it shall save us much conflict and unrest. And that shall be more than a payment to me." He forwarded three tickets to Poltu and the latter thanked him.

Poltu said gently, "Sir, we need a ticket for our Bahadur too."

"Bahadur? Who is he?", asked the conductor.

Dholki said in her sweet voice, "He is our puppy, our friend through thick and thin; he is sleeping under your seat as he is going without a ticket."

"I see!", said the conductor.

Just then the person sitting at the back of the bus shouted, "Oh my God, I shall die!"

Everyone was startled and looked at him. The dog had caught hold of his leg. There was a wad of notes below his feet. The conductor looked at him and understood the matter. Few notes from his bag had fallen off and the man had been trying to take it. Bahadur had got hold of the notes with his feet.

Once the conductor picked up the notes, Bahadur let go of his feet and again fell asleep like a good boy. The conductor said gladly, "Bahadur had paid many times his price of ticket by catching the thief. Otherwise, I would have had to bail out so much money. Bahadur is a loyal friend of yours. Just as you are very good children, he is a very good friend of yours."

Everyone got down at the end of a city. There was a big hotel right in front. The smell of the food whetted the appetite of the children. They became just too hungry when they remembered they had not had anything since morning. But there was no money with them. What to do? They saw few children were standing near the hotel just asking for money in the name of piety appealing to the kindness of people passing by.

Should they also ask for money to eat? No, when they had the strength to do work, they could not beg. It was better to work and earn and eat. They saw children even smaller than them were serving and cleaning the utensils in the hotel. There was no shame in this, in working and earning. They were children just like them. Great people were never ashamed to work for themselves. In this country, even Ishwar Chandra Vidyasagar had not hesitated to do the job of a porter. Father of the Nation, Mahatma Gandhi had explained well the dignity of labour. He was cleaning the garbage. They were the children of this country. If they did not have money with them, it was much more respectable to do hard work and earn than stealing, begging or cheating. Hard work should ward off hunger. But right now, hunger was acute, and where was the time to work and earn?

The pangs of hunger were so acute that they sat down and ordered for food as if they had money with them. They could not think more. They ate to their heart's content and fed Bahadur too. Once they ate to their fill, they thought of paying to the hotel. The shop keeper was sitting with his big belly and looking at them keenly!

The children just could not escape his burning eyes glancing at them.

Seeing their unsettled ways, he had already guessed the problem. Many such children had already given the names and addresses of their parents earlier. Sometimes, the whereabouts of the parents were wrong too.

Often the parents used to get angry. They might say on being asked for money, "Did you ask me when you fed the children on credit? Is there any proof that my children had eaten? You are encouraging these habits in children. You should have first seen if they have money with them or not." Then the shopkeeper was nonplussed. He could not run the shop by first asking for money, before feeding people. These were varied experiences of shopkeepers. He told gravely, "Children, pay your bill. Why are you puzzled? If you cannot do it, come. I am finalizing the calculations."

Oltu looked at Paltu. Paltu looked at Dholki. Dholki was scared. What a matter of shame! There was no money with them. But they had already eaten. Paltu winked at Oltu and he in turn winked at Dholki. The shopkeeper felt that, within the blink of an eye, they would start to run like hawks away from there. He thought-

"But how far can they go, this girl with unkempt hair cannot not run fast and up to what distance can they run, let me see!" The shopkeeper was alert. But what did the children do suddenly? Both the brothers started to lift the dishes from tables and started to clean those below the water tap. Dholki began to clean the tables. The hotelier was struck still. Such beautiful children and they seemed to be from some gentry. They did not have money right then and had eaten out of hunger.

But should they work like this to pay? He stopped them and told- "No, no. You are students, and you are not to do this work here. Do not demean your parents. My payment is deemed to be done. Many children like you eat in credit everyday taking pleas and dropping names. And if I ask for money, they say the Government shall pay for them. Are we given employment so that we may pay? You are, in contrast, quite small and innocent children."

Oltu said gently, "To do labour to earn and satisfy the needs is not demeaning, Sir. It does not insult one, rather adds to one's dignity. Parents shall be happy, not ashamed to know this. If you waive it, that shall be a shame. Allow us to work."

Paltu said sweetly, "We are not reading just to get a job from the Government. We are studying to be good citizens, to use brain and brawn to earn, to keep up the honour of the country and the nation while doing our own upkeep. We shall not talk like those cheating children to you."

The hotelier was moved to tears. He thought, "Such genuinely good children were also there. But sometimes we generalize about the younger generation so negatively! These children have been groomed well by their parents and obey their teachers. There are many such good children in the country. We think ill of all because of few disorderly fellows. Such noble children can surely lead others away from wrong path to the right one."

He was happy and thought, "Let them work if they are doing so happily. Students earning by cleaning the plates is not something mean. It is rather noble a work. Because of our narrow ideas, we feel bad about good things and become small." The children cleaned the tables, the dishes, and the room. They fetched water from the tap. All were taken by surprise. All had good words for them. The wicked children who had come to eat without paying felt ashamed and left in silence. Some joined them in doing the chores. They cleaned the cobwebs, and made the floor look slick. The nearby roads and drains were all cleaned. The doors and windows were scrubbed and looked new. The get-up was brushed up and there was a fresh look. Everything began to shine. People started to sit and eat joyfully. The hotelier was happy too. Payment for food was done. He paid them money too for expenses on the way back. The lessons that the small maestros taught was indeed invaluable. So precious that no money can measure it!

In the Den of Dacoits

The three children set out for home with money in pocket and joy in heart. Bahadur, as usual, was leading the way. As if he knew all the ways around the world.

A blind boy was walking in the middle of the road, feeling his way. Oltu held his hand and guided him across the road. He asked, "Brother, where shall you go? If you wish, I shall book a ticket for you in a bus. We have more money

with us than what we need to get back home."
At this time, a boy who was limping came near
them. Dholki became kind and gave a coin to
him. Paltu got angry with Dholki and
reprimanded her, "Dholki, don't you know
normal courtesy? He is just a child like us. His
legs may be impaired. But he has two hands, eyes,
ears, and brain. And he has intelligence, just like
us. Nowadays there are schools and colleges for
them. The blind, deaf and mute are reading like
others and taking up jobs. They are earning for
themselves and tending to families too. They do
not need the pity and sympathy from others. How
would you feel if someone gives money to you in
pity? We know now there is not much difference
between us and them. They are human like us
and can live with dignity."

The behaviour and words moved the two
children to tears. The limping child took a wary
look around and told them, "Brother, we were
also hale and hearty like you. We belonged to good
families and were studying in a school. We too
had affection, compassion, and more such feelings
in our hearts. But everything changed all on a
sudden. We became blind and disabled. Some of

us do not have an eye, some have lost limbs like a hand or a leg. Few have lost their tongue."

"How did it all happen? Who did this to you?" Dholki asked with tears in her eyes.

The blind boy mumbled, "Child-catchers caught us. We were also roaming around on the roads without heeding the words of our parents."

"Why did he do this to you?" Paltu was concerned.

The small boy said, "This is their way of earning money. They shall become rich by thus exploiting us."

Dholki was surprised, "Maiming the human children, one shall earn money? This is way too cruel and strange!"

The blind boy said sadly, "Yes, Sister! They are earning money through us. They get hold of many healthy boys and girls and make them handicapped. Then they are left on the road to beg. Kind people give them money. The money goes to these dacoits, and we get few pieces of rotten bread. If we take healthy food, our fit condition cannot make people feel kind. So, we move ill-fed and ill-clad on the roads. This is our life. We have almost forgotten our homes and near and dear ones. Children, go back home early. The spies of dacoits are after us. You should not come to their notice now. We do not want brothers and sisters of our country to be in our condition. Let them study, grow up and work for themselves and the country."

Dholki was crying already. Oltu and Paltu also had tears in their eyes.

Oltu whispered to them, "Brothers, come with us. We shall make you reach your homes."

The blind boy said, "Our houses are far away. Spies are keeping a watch on us. If we arouse their suspicion, death awaits us. You shall also be in the danger of losing your precious lives. We might somehow escape with you. But what shall happen to hundreds like us who are in their hold and suffering day in and day out. We cannot leave them in this cave of death and go away. Think if you can do something to redress this wrong as a whole."

Oltu and Paltu were moved to think on this. They thought it would be a matter of shame to see this condition of hundreds of children and get back to the comfort and safety of their home and parents, without doing anything for the lot of these hapless children. They were not keen to feel satisfied by dropping a coin or two in the hands of these children on the roads. Rather, they should rise to the occasion by tackling these evil people and addressing the wrongs. This evil business must end. First, they must get at the den of these dacoits. But how to do that? They asked the two children in trust. The children were too afraid, "Brother, don't step into the trap now! You cannot get back into freedom once you get there. Our lives are already condemned. Why should you suffer like this for us?"

Oltu told him, "Brother, your life is not done for. First, you must set yourselves free from this. Then, you shall have treatment. There are many modern systems of education for you. You can be healthy again. We can donate an eye each to people like you. All of us shall be well." They agreed to be part of the adventure. As per their advice, Oltu became blind, Paltu limped and Dholki became a dumb girl! They acted so well like children with disabilities! Now they could easily mix up with the crowd of these children and walk back to the den of dacoits. They would have to leave Bahadur behind. Handsome and furry Bahadur would surely raise the suspicion of the dacoits. But how to leave him aside when he was such a fine friend in need?

Bahadur was following their words, as it were. Suddenly he began to limp and drag himself. They were so happy with his acting. But his healthy and handsome look would raise a question for sure-how come the dog of three beggar children was so winsome?

"Then what to do?", Oltu asked.

"That is what I am thinking. We can't leave him behind", Paltu said.

Then Dholki ventured suddenly, "Then, do what I say."

"Let us see then. What is your idea?" teased Paltu.

Dholki said if we cut away Bahadur's furs at random, he should look famished.

Yes, that was true. All agreed. Paltu took him to a roadside barber and had his hair trimmed in an unkempt and ugly way. The healthy and handsome dog looked so awkward and unclean now. All were a little sad to see him in his new guise.

Oltu pleaded, "Well, when our job is done, we shall again groom his hairs and make him nice. The outward appearance is not the real thing, it is the quality within that matters. Father of the Nation, Mahatma Gandhi was wearing a dhoti hardly covering his knees and using an indigenous simple shawl and the sahibs used to call him a barbarian and a half-naked fakir. But that naked fakir, without a war, could drive them away from this country in a non-violent struggle and became the Father of the Nation. We shall follow his example." All were happy now.

All of them walked to the den of the dacoits. The jungle started where the town ended.

It was close to evening. Four big men looking like hooligans came out from the forest. Paltu asked, "Who are they?".

The boy with a limp told, "They are spies who keep a watch on us. They shall now blindfold us and take us to their den so that we are never ever able to come back or escape on our own. You all must be cautious right from here."

Oltu immediately started to act blind. Paltu became lame. Dholki was looking dull and acted dumb. Bahadur went ahead of them and walked dragging his legs.

The spies of the dacoits surrounded them. They looked sternly at them and asked about them.

The lame boy replied, "They were also begging like us. The three siblings are blind, lame and dumb. Even their companion dog has become lame. They are homeless orphans, having lost everything in a flood. They survived, as luck would have it, as they had been to their maternal uncle's. The uncle and aunt too have turned them away after their parents have been taken away by the flood. Now they are begging and living homeless, lying under the shade of wild trees in sun and shower. We have called them to our place so that they would stay with us. Whatever they fetch they shall give to the Master. And they shall live with us here."

The spies believed the words, they patted their back and told, "Very good. If we get such children in this natural way, why would we kidnap urchins and maim them? Why would we hack their limbs to make them lame?"

Oltu, while walking with closed eyes and

groping his way, said, "Sir, we have many friends like us. They are reading in the school of the blind, deaf and dumb. If you say, we shall also bring the teachers with us. It is because of the teachers that the children, instead of begging on the road, are reading there. If the teachers are not there, all shall mingle with us and beg happily."

Another spy joined in, "That is right. What these handicapped boys and girls shall do, studying in a school? Rather if they join us, they shall get two pieces of bread to eat everyday evening. What shall they do if they just sit inside the society?"

Paltu could hardly control himself. He was thinking of spurting out, "The differently abled should not be kept away from the society. They are a part and parcel of this society. They can work and live like the normal people, if given the education and opportunity. They are not helpless and can play a role in the positive works in the nation. The differently abled should also look upon themselves as worthy."

Even with all these thoughts, Paltu stayed silent. Now is the time for action. If he speaks out, all shall be ending in smoke. So, he continued to walk in silence.

All reached the den. The Master was very happy to see the new members. But he advised his followers to be discreet and watchful about these new fellows.

The days became difficult for Oltu, Paltu and Dholki. They were begging all day and eating a little in the evening. Even Bahadur could hardly eat those breads! But they had to take the pain. History records that there is enough pain and sacrifice behind many good works in the world. How could they back out now?

One day, Oltu, by chance collided with a blind boy on the road. As it is, Oltu acts blind, so might have missed his steps. That boy said- "Brother, excuse me! I can't see the way. I have not pushed you willingly. I am in the school of the blind. I am now in the final year in the school."

Oltu, holding his hand, told happily, "Brother, I am also blind. I am begging on the road. I am also sad to have hit you unknowingly.

The boy said with some sadness in his voice, "Brother, why are you begging? You can very well study and be able to earn. The differently abled are becoming well trained and experts in so many things. You come with me. Get admitted to the school and study."

Oltu requested him, "Brother, rather you come with me. Then you shall help us in rescuing such children from hell. I am not actually handicapped. But I am acting."

The boy became astonished. Paltu told the whole story. The student of the school for blind, Mohan became willing to accompany Oltu and others to the den of dacoits. He could teach few other children there. He could find a way out for them. Happiness does not come to one when one is surrounded by unhappy people. To bear a bit of pain to make others happy is the real happiness. That is why the twelve-year-old Dharmapada jumped into the sea to save twelve hundred workmen.

Studies in the Den

Studies begin in the den at night after the dacoits become drunk post dinner. Oltu, Paltu and Dholki taught the small ones as per their ability and Mohan started teaching the blind children. They had come to realize that study is the best companion for self-defense, for tackling the dangers and for solution of problems in the struggle of life. They were also on the lookout for bringing the dacoits to book, apart from progressing in their studies. But they never got an occasion to go to the police station and report. The spies were always after them. One day the trio hit upon an idea. Oltu gave a thrashing to Bahadur without any apparent reason. Paltu shouted, "Get out, get out from here!" Dholki said, "Get this dog out of here." The leader of the dacoits asked in surprise, "What happened? Why are you beating your friend, the little dog?"

Oltu said, "Nowadays he is not listening to us. Only taking a share of food and getting idle by the day. What is the fun in keeping an idle lame dog with us?"

The Master said, "Yeah, that is true. Then shoot him down."

Dholki joined her palms, "Sir, why do a dirty thing like hurting a shrew. Why to waste a precious bullet for a dying dog? Rather if we shoot a deer or a boar, it shall be a great feast."

The leader was happy, "That is great. You are intelligent. Then drive away the dog. Let me go hunting. Tonight, we shall have a grand feast!"

Paltu kicked the dog away and saw him off

at a distance from there. Poor Bahadur kept crying and whining and dragged himself away, as if not knowing a bit about what was happening all around.

Mohan was worried and asked Oltu in a whispering tone, "Brother, what did you do? How can you drive away the friend of your weal and woe in such a way?"

Paltu said in the same whispering tone, "Bahadur has gone to the uncle's house. Uncle shall come with his friends."

'Means?', Mohan was surprised.

Oltu said, "I have put a map of the den with a letter in his mouth. Bahadur knows my commands. He shall straight go to the police station. When the dacoits shall be sleeping after their feast tonight, then they shall be surrounded. All shall be caught."

Mohan was mighty happy.

The spies had an eye on Bahadur. Bahadur limped his way up to the brink of the forest. He looked back and was sure that no one was following him. Then like a good dog he jumped and danced his way ahead. But the spies had seen it all. They came back and told the gang-leader.

The leader too came to know that the three kids, just like Bahadur were not handicapped at all. There must be a secret behind their coming. They decided that night to burn everything down and shift the camp. Else, everything was risky for them.

There was a feast in the evening. All the children were fed well. The Leader was telling himself, "Eat well, urchins. This is your last meal. Your cleverness is known to us, and you shall all die now. We shall get many other children. We shall get hold of normal children and maim them. It is not a big deal for us."

Bahadur came limping at the time of the feast. He took shelter near Dholki who commented innocently, "The shameless dog has come again attracted by the smell of mutton. Even after all the beatings and kicking. Greedy One!"

One dacoit teased, "Well, when he has come, feed him well. His legs shall be fine, fully healed when there is a foment by fire tonight."

The children were unaware that the dacoits would burn them down that night. The dacoits were not knowing either, that the police would surround them that night. Both were happy in their own thoughts, dacoits got more drunk in their own secret joy. Dholki had put on trinkets and jingles and was dancing to keep the dacoits happy and unaware. The dacoits were clapping and laughing a lot. Right then Bahadur smelled something and stood still.

There was the smell of petrol all around. By this time the dacoits had poured the fuel in different places. After a while they would throw a burning matchstick and retreat into safety. And the children should be caught in the fire. Bahadur smelt it and gave a bite to Oltu's legs. It was a signal. Oltu and Paltu became alert. They also smelt it. Bahadur started dancing more as if giving the signal to them to flee when he was keeping a watch. Even though they thought of the dear dog, they had to save now the life of the children all around. If the fire came up suddenly, they could not flee. So, compromising the life of the dog, Dholki, Paltu and Oltu started to dance their way to a far-off point and the lame boys, holding the hands of the blind ones, gradually edged their way out of the forest. In the fun filled dance and the intoxication, the dacoits were unable to know what exactly was coming about.

Near the jungle was the vast sea. Two motor launches were anchored on the beach. Oltu, Paltu and Dholki got into a launch. The children followed them. There was the sound of the siren of the police jeep and the dacoits running after them. The all-consuming flame of the fire was also visible from a distance. Quite a few drunk dacoits got burnt in that fire.

The Leader and a few dacoits got into the other launch in the meantime. By then, the launch of the children was already sailing in the sea.

Danger upon Danger

Few children were knowing how to drive a launch. As the dacoits were deploying them in all sorts of work, they had this knack of knowing different things. The vessel sailed on followed by the one of the dacoits. The launch was oscillating with the waves of the sea. It felt as if the vessel would be upset any moment. The dacoits were steering their launch in an unsteady drunk manner. They could not get near the children as much as they tried. The gang-leader then took out the gun and trained it upon the children. He thought if he could shoot the driver of the vessel with children, the launch would capsize. It was all visible from their vessel. And they were deep in prayers. Right then the dacoit leader gave out a cry and fell. The children saw one black animal had mauled the shooting arms of the fallen dacoit.

The dacoit driving the launch got nervous and unsettled in all this hullabaloo and suddenly the launch hit a big rock and broke up. It was a sudden and watery grave for the two dacoits, an apt reward for their evil deeds. All others had been engulfed in the fire. Some more might have been nabbed by the police. The children were assured now. But they were not happy exactly. They sat down and prayed for the peace of their souls. Even though they were dacoits, they were human beings. How can they rejoice in the death of other humans?

Suddenly all remembered Bahadur too. Poor dog! He had sacrificed his life to save them. They pined for him. There were tears in the eyes of

Dholki. Right then a piece of broken boat was sailing towards their vessel. And that black animal was sitting atop it. This animal only has saved them now. They would surely rescue it. They threw a rope unto that sailing block of wood. The animal gave a bite and clung to it. And the children slowly roped him in.

Wow! it was their dear friend Bahadur!

Furs of Bahadur had got burnt up in the fire and had become black. His appearance had become so ugly! He had followed the dacoits in this semi-burnt state and had hidden in the boat without their knowledge. And he saved their lives! Even if he was burnt, he was alive! That was great joy to them.

All were eager to tend to Bahadur. There was always some food and necessary items in the launches of dacoits. And wine too. Two raw eggs were given to Bahadur to gulp down. And some brandy. Bahadur kept trembling as he was in the cold waters of the sea. The children applied their mind, but the brandy was a little too much for him. Now what shall the children do? Bahadur was drunk and he began dancing. Dholki had put Burnol on his burnt body. He was looking part white, part black and part yellow. His strange dance looked stranger with his multi-coloured body. The children burst into laughter. Oltu sounded grave, "Comrades, we are all sailing in the sea. We never know where we all shall reach and what we shall face. In this condition we should not be in fun and frolic without thinking for the future. Enjoyment shall come, but not now."

Children were not paying any heed. They had come out of the clutches of dacoits after so many days. Blue sea was all around. Azure sky was above them. Nothing else was visible, this apart. They were free. The worry for future had no place now in the newfound joy of freedom!

Dholki took Bahadur to her lap and was trying to put him to sleep, patting him. She started to sing. As if she was not a little girl, but a caring old aunt. Bahadur fell asleep. Dholki said like a guardian, "Who gave so much brandy to Bahadur, when so much medicine is with us. That which makes people mad, should not be touched even by us. How many lives, property and families are ruined in our country because of the influence of these intoxicants! People are falling victims of irremediable diseases. There is so much untimely death. A man near our home died a few days back. His kith and kin are seething without food and drinks now." Dholki tossed all the bottles, one by one, into the sea. The waves kept dancing. As if they had become inebriate with the liquor. All the children made sit ups holding their ears, as if in punishment and vowed that in future after growing up too, they would not touch wine or alcohol. Rather they would persuade people not to drink and de-addict the ones who drink.

Terrible Danger

All on a sudden, Paltu shouted, "Alas, what shall we do now?". Everyone looked at him. None could get him at first. His two eyes had become enlarged, in fear. He was looking at a corner of the launch. There was a small hole in the corner and the sea water was slowly seeping into their vessel. There were bullets, shot by the dacoits, which had made a hole there. Now what was to be done? The launch might go down midway. They saved themselves from dacoits. But now the sea shall engulf them all. All became agitated. But Oltu assured them, "Don't be restless now. If we panic, danger shall grow. Let us think of ways out of this. Die if we must, we shall die, but why shall we not try to live?"

All were a little patient now. Oltu started searching the things. Paltu tried to join hands. The dacoits must have kept some tools or something. Water kept on seeping into the vessel and the children were so scared.

Suddenly Paltu shouted, "Eureka, Eureka!" Everyone's eyes were now fixed on him. There was a hammer in his hand. Oltu had got some nails and metal plates. The two brothers made a patch on the hole with the hammer and the nails. Just as people put patches in the bucket and metal pots. They had seen it at their home. Now they applied it here. They put fire on wax candles and applied the liquid wax around the patch to seal it. Then there was no water seeping anymore.

Now the launch was safe and steady. Oltu and Paltu were profusely thanked by the children. But they said, "Thank the Lord. He only helps the humans and guides them to do the right things in grave situations to wriggle out of danger."

In a New World

After the danger was over, all were thinking about the way ahead. They could not keep sailing on the sea like this! The store of food was getting depleted. All were eating less and drinking less. If they did not ration and share well, all might lose their lives on board. Suddenly Dholki began to dance with joy. All were eager to know the reason of her delight. Dholki pointed the finger and when they looked their joy knew no bounds. They saw the line of coconut trees and hills on the distant horizon. As if they were waving their arms and welcoming the children. They thought they shall reach the land soon and there should be human beings there. And civilization. They could think of returning to their home and hearth from there. The launch was moving on, dancing with the waves of the sea. Gradually, the hills and the trees were becoming clearer. As if these were not the trees, but guards standing there to protect the country from invaders.

The short coconut trees were laden with lot of fruits. The golden yellow coconuts were quite tempting. But no buildings were visible till then. The children thought that houses may be far off, so not readily visible. But they were sure that they shall quickly reach the shore.

The nearer they got to land, the happier they became. Suddenly there was a storm in the offing, the blue sky became black. The waters of the sea became blacker than even the clouded sky. The launch was shaking in the storm. It felt as if it would capsize any moment, and the children would be eaten up by the ferocious sea. Bahadur had still not recovered. Dholki was holding him close. She felt if the launch is capsized, she would be holding onto Bahadur to save him from the aggressive waves.

The lunch made its way slowly towards the land despite the storm. The shore was getting nearer. If they tide over this storm, they should be safe. The children kept looking at the shore, breathless and eager. The land was looking at them like a mother extending her arms to take them to her lap.

They were getting nearer. But suddenly the launch was getting drawn to a hillock. Within moments it would hit the rock and break into splinters. The speed of the vessel was beyond control as if a mighty demon was dragging it.

The children were praying, "Oh God, if the launch veers a bit away from the rocks, we shall reach the shore and so many innocent lives shall be saved."

But what happened now! The launch hit the rocks and was shattered into pieces. Oltu, Paltu, Dholki and all others were scattered suddenly. All closed their eyes in fear. It was darkness all around. Pitch dark!

Surprise in an Unknown Island

Oltu opened his eyes first. Paltu was clinging to him, holding him tight. He was not conscious. Both were on the shore. And they were alive. Oltu dragged Paltu to a dry place. None was nearby, no medicines too, to bring back him to senses. Oltu gave a massage to Paltu's palms and feet. He made it warm by pressing it again and again. Paltu came back to senses. On opening the eyes, he enquired, "Where is Dholki and Bahadur?"

Oltu said sadly, "Not only those two, but none of our team is also perhaps alive. All are lost in the sea. By chance, we are on the shore. But let us see in the morning who else are there around here. Let us be patient."

Paltu was all tears for his sister. And for all others. But the words of Oltu made him patient and he felt like waiting for daybreak.

It was dark. Nothing was visible, no human habitat, no houses. The two brothers were huddled into a cave-like corner on the shore. Day broke. They found that they were sitting in a beautiful island. All around the trees were full of fruits and flowers. Birds were singing. But there was no sign of humans or houses. They seemed to be owners of this enchanting island. There was none to snatch away this lovely island with its fruits and flowers, flora and fauna, fountains and rivers. But they could not be happy with this thought. Can man ever be happy with wealth and luxury if the kith and kin and companions and society are not there with one? They took some ripe banana; other fruits being unknown to them, they did not touch those. Then they set out to search for others marooned in the shipwreck. Moving by the shore they saw a big portion of the vessel was stuck on the rock. Big waves of the sea were not able to carry it away. Oltu could make out that the hillock had magnet in it and was pulling the vessels towards it. They saw another old ship lying broken a furlong away. That ship had become junk.

In the big broken portion of their launch all were sitting with heads down and in mortal fear. Hearing the voices, all came out of the vessel. Oltu and Paltu were happy. But Dholki and Bahadur were nowhere in sight. Maybe they had drowned in the sea.

All were sad for Dholki and Bahadur. Oltu and Paltu were utterly sad for their darling sister, but mustered courage to face it all. There was no other way too. They were in doubt if Dholki was alive or not. All of them moved in a group. First, they had to know about this island. Then they would see what could be done.

Man-eating Man

After moving on for a distance, they saw a heap of white things were piled up in one place. When they went closer, they were pale with shock.

All were human bones. Skulls, skeletons, hands, legs and all! Wherefrom humans came to this distant land? Who had kept these piled up? If animals would have eaten them, the bones should not be stacked up in this way. Then …? They were struck with mortal fear now. They had heard that cannibals still lived in this world. Perhaps they had reached such an island where the humans had not seen the light of education and civilization. Maybe they had devoured the men struck in the shipwrecks there and piled up the bones here. Had Dholki been a victim of these cannibals? Both the brothers were in tears now.

Right then a small boy shouted, "Look Brother, there is a red flag flying at a distance. There must be a temple there and the people in the island must be civilized." They all marched in that direction. Before that they tied their broken launch and the ship on the shore to the hillock, so that these would not sail away. Because there were many items in store in those two.

When they went near the flag, Paltu screamed in joy, "Oh Brother, our Dholki is alive and well!" Others could not understand. Paltu said, "This red flag is nothing but the frock of Dholki. She is signalling about her presence." All nodded their heads in consent and started to walk faster now. Paltu directed the differently abled children to rest on a plain patch as it was difficult for them to walk in the hilly tracts.

Oltu and Paltu walked fast and reached the spot. They found that it was in fact, the frock of Dholki which was tied to a long pole. Bahadur was standing holding the other end of the pole with his two front legs, just like a human child! When he saw them, he left it and ran to them, jumping in joy. He then led the way. Dholki was lying on a broken block of the launch and was trembling in cold. Bahadur had jumped unto the shore and come, but as it was not possible for her to jump and thus come to shore, she had given her frock to him with a long floating pole which she got hold of. Bahadur has understood the signal of Dholki and acted.

The two brothers used the pole as a prop to drag the block of floating wood to the shore and as soon as it reached, they pulled up Dholki holding her hands.

The two brothers embraced Dholki and were crying with joy. Then all three of them came back to the plain area where other children were resting. There were lot of plants with fruits and flowers. Coconuts and bananas aplenty. All ate bananas and drank coconut water breaking those with stone. Green was the colour with verdant scene all around. The island looked like a green fairy and the clear waters of rivers and fountains were like her pearl necklaces. They named it the 'Green Island'.

The Miracle of the Fruit of Laughter

Then all moved around exploring the island. There was no trace of humans or their habitation. But cows, goats and cocks and hens were freely moving around in the forest. Children had become tired. Another side of the forest remained untouched. Humans might be there on that side. Suddenly Dholki picked up a red fruit from an unknown plant. Before she could take it to her mouth, Bahadur jumped to snatch it away from her. They could know Bahadur was telling, "Just as one should not befriend one seeing the outward appearance, one should not eat a fruit seeing its attractive look. This may be poisonous too."

Bahadur sniffed the fruit, licked it, then out of greed he too started to taste it and ate it up. Then he started grinning mad-like and rolled with laughter. He was rolling on the ground as if someone was tickling him. All were astonished. What was to be done now? How could a dog laugh like humans? Paltu said, "This is the Laughter Fruit. One may feel butterflies and tickles if one eats this. Maybe after some time he shall become alright." He became still and motionless after some time. After a bit of patting, again he walked normally with joy and pride. After some time, they saw a clean space where the upper portions of trees from both sides had been pulled together and tied like buns of hair. There was a big cave nearby. That meant humans were there. There were weapons of iron and stone and bows and arrows. There are piles of human bones and skeletons too.

They could understand man-eating men were living in that area. They hid atop the big trees. The children who could not walk or see returned to the plain area near the shore. Their main work was to build a few houses to live. Mohan from the Blind School accompanied them. Now he would teach them lessons. Oltu, Paltu and Dholki were recognized as maestros. They remained along with Bahadur to befriend the inhabitants of this island.

All remained hidden in the cover of tall trees. Now the forest people came there. They had covered themselves with barks. They were hale and hearty and harsh in their looks and had brought with them a dead bullock and a dead pig. They skinned those animals and started to eat the raw flesh. Then they took out the laughter fruit, ate it and became intoxicated and rolled on the ground. In their bizarre laughter, Dholki began to shiver in fear. Oltu said, "Don't fear, now you have to do a lot."

The jungle people sat around a big rock

which was smeared with red colour and was garlanded. They began to sing sitting around the rock. That was their chanting or prayer.

In the meantime, Oltu and Paltu had decked up Dholki with garlands and applied white marks on her head. Dholki got down from the tree and went and sat hiding behind the rock they were worshipping.

Just then a snake slithered in. The forest people got up in fear seeing it. They were thinking it to be a messenger from God. Right then Dholki came out and she started singing and dancing there. Oltu played on a flute and Paltu struck two stones like two parts of a cymbal. The snake began to sway and dance to the rhythm of this music. The jungle people were struck with surprise. They thought these were messengers from the Gods and Dholki was Banadurga*. Dholki continued to sing and dance till the snake had disappeared into the forests. The music of the flute of Oltu held them spell bound. Some dancing to its tune. They had become in a way enthralled by the three children. Some said in their language, "These are the Gods of forests. We shall

---

Goddess of the forest

worship them." Another group of people said, "God or human, the flesh of these must be tender and delicious. We shall eat them." Another said, "No, these are our rulers. We shall abide by their direction." A few others said, "Let us test their intelligence and their strength." All agreed to that. But some others insisted on killing and eating them. Arguments ensued and there was conflict. Tempers flared, there was mutual scolding and beating.

Oltu, Paltu and Dholki did not understand their language, but understood their signs and gestures and intentions, all. They suddenly hit upon an idea. They sat there like fixed statues. One had put hands on eyes, another on the ears and the third one, on the mouth. They sat like the three monkeys of the Father of the Nation, Gandhiji. They were still, immobile for few moments. The jungle people were surprised and leaving aside their conflicts looked at them. They asked them the meaning of this posture through their signs.

Dholki explained through sign language that they had come from India and the Father of the Nation had told "Do not see evil, don't hear evil, don't speak evil." You are all using evil language and behaving badly with each other. We shall not participate in that. We shall surely join you if you do good work."

The jungle people understood her expression as she had already mastered the art in doing so in the den of dacoits.

All of them sat quiet. Some of them had hands on their eyes. Some, on their ears and some on their mouths. There was peace. Then Oltu signaled to them that they had come to befriend them. Their leader communicated that they should first test the brain and brawn of these children. Oltu, Paltu and Dholki agreed to that.

Fight with the Giant-Head

The magnetic hill which caused accidents in the sea was known as the Giant-head to these jungle people. Because when they went near it, their iron weapons were all snatched away by the hill. They could not retrieve the weapons from the hills, try as they might. So, they thought the hill to be a demon. It had become a hill with the curse of someone, but its might had not diminished, they thought.

That was ideal place to test the strength of Oltu and Paltu. That was their decision. The two brothers had read about magnetism in the school. They knew magnet attracts only iron. So, they made two swords in wood and smeared black colour on that. In the vessel there were knives of steel too. That was also brought. Then both the sides went near the Giant-head. When the jungle people tried to attack Oltu and Paltu, their weapons were attracted by the hill. But the wooden swords and the steel knives of the boys was still in their hands. And they also struck the hill with their swords. That made the forest folk dumb and spell bound. They fell flat at the feet of the three children. Oltu and Paltu lifted them and shook hands and told them they were all friends and equals. The people were very happy then.

Bahadur was barking bravely as if it could overcome even a tiger if it sees one.

Right then, some langurs came down from the hill. Like the jungle people, they were also looking stocky and terrific. The jungle folk were afraid of the langurs, because the monkeys used to tear the face and bodies of people. They began running helter-skelter now. But Bahadur chased the monkeys away boldly. The big monkeys ran back with their tails between their legs and got up the trees and hid their faces. Bahadur was walking on proudly like a great hero. The Jungle people were now following him meekly.

After a while the forest became thicker. The day looked like the night. The terrific sound of the animals was heard. The people searched for their weapons, lest there might be a tiger or a

lion. Bahadur was walking proudly thinking of the monkeys. Suddenly a jungle cat came out. Bahadur beat retreat in haste. He hit a rock and fell unconscious. Oltu and Paltu were also bursting into laughter. Oltu sprinkled water on Bahadur's face and told him slowly when he regained senses, "Bahadur, it is not good to show off one's strength and capacity too much. It is always better to do something and then take credit. From today, don't make yourself a laughing stock". Bahadur, with twinkling eyes listened to him, as if he understood everything. He drank a lot of water. And then he started to walk slowly.

Demon-fruit and the River of Milk and Curd

The island was full of coconut trees, but the local people were not taking it. They did not know that it was an edible item. They called it the demon-fruit. Many years ago, a man had died walking below such a tree when he was hit in the head. Then onwards, the coconut was called the demon fruit, and the tree was a ghost tree for them. They said the ghost tree calls everyone to it and those who go near it die, beaten by him. The branches, when dry and long look that way and all these trees were laden with coconuts too. Sometimes the coconuts fall, and the people referred to that as the blow of the tree.

When Oltu and Paltu walked towards the trees, the jungle people tried to dissuade them. The brothers assured them of their safety and went near the trees. The people were afraid and watched them from a distance. Oltu and Paltu brought out some coconuts from short trees, took out the coir, broke them, drank the water of tender coconut and ate the coconut. Bahadur drank the water of four tender green coconuts. The coconut water is very sweet. The jungle people thought that these children would become drunk or die. But when nothing happened to them, the jungle folk also mustered courage and drank the water and ate the fruit. They became so happy that they lifted Oltu, Paltu and Dholki and danced. They also recognized the trio as Maestros.

After some time, they found a river whose water was white like milk. There were lot of cheese and milk in that. They found many healthy cows and buffaloes. Milk was flowing from their udders. The children understood that the people there had not learnt to take milk and curd, but only the flesh of the animals.

All three now took milk from the river and ate cheese and curd with joy. The milk was becoming cheese and flowing on. Bahadur too jumped into the river and drank a lot of milk. He was about to drown. He had drunk so much that he was hardly able to swim. Paltu gave him two blows and picked him up from the river. He cautioned, "The result of greed is death. Be warned." The jungle people too started to drink milk and take cheese. They yawned happily. They liked the intelligence of these children.

Tackling a Burning Snake

The special children were busy on the other side of the island in making houses. Oltu, Paltu and Dholki took the forest folk and walked towards that side. It was evening. There was fire on one side of the forest. A few trees caught fire. There was a beauty in that spark of lights in the night. As if it was a light decoration for a wedding or festival. Right then, a fiery snake ran down from the upper hills. The jungle people feared the snake and took it as a god. Burning snake was still more fearsome to them. They believed if God gets angry, forests caught fire and burning snakes came out of the forest. They shouted in fear. A jungle snake came down and was lying still on the plain. They thought it would burn them up. Oltu told them not to worry, fetched water from the nearby fountain and poured it on the snake. The snake died instantly and lay there. The jungle people raised their eyebrows and looked with amazement. This boy was so brave and smart! He controlled the burning snake god just with some water.

Oltu knew a burning snake shall never come down so smoothly over the hills. If it catches fire, the snake shall suffer. There may be iron uphill. Melting in fire, the iron is coming down beautifully. When water is poured the burning iron becomes cold and hard and is brought back to its immobile metallic state. If heated, the solid becomes liquid, and if cooled, the liquid becomes solid. Matter has three conditions, solid, liquid, and gaseous. Putting his knowledge got through books to use, Oltu got accolades from the forest folk.

A New Society in a New World

Then all came together and reached the other children who were busy in making houses. But how surprising! There were rows of neat houses standing in the solitary island. The walls were smeared with red and black earth. The dumb girls had created lovely patterns in white powder. To ward off the wild animals fencing had been done with thorny plants.

The forest people wondered how much they had suffered under sun and showers. Using the earth, stones, grass, wood, bamboo, and leaves the children had made such beautiful houses like ace craftsmen. They were so intelligent even though younger in age. They were the teachers. Now they accepted these little ones as their guides. They also started building houses. Within a few days the forest area became a beautiful village.

They did not know agriculture. They were foraging food and hunting. Oltu and Paltu thought it would be a good idea to teach them the basics of agriculture. They brought seedling with earth and planted them in one place and watered them. The gardens started to bloom with fruits and were now enchanting orchards. The jungle people were strong and hardworking. The main thing was to motivate them to work well. That motivation was done by the three kids. They also started to rear cows and goats at home. They learnt to make salt out of the sea water. There were wild cotton trees in the forest. These were just growing. Mohan taught them all how to spin clothes out of these. They made clothes and wore them. By and by, a peaceful and harmonious society came up there.

Seniors go to School

Then the main concern was school and studies for the islanders. Oltu, Paltu and Dholki had studied a bit. Mohan too had studied. They started a school, and the children of the jungle started to study there. Dholki started the lessons on Odishi song and dance there. She also started to learn their songs and dances. All tried to learn manual work too. Mohan was quite adept in this.

Carpentry was taught there. Mats were made. Works of jute and brooms also found a place. The people were happy. The black earth was burnt, and slates were made. From white stone, chalks were made. The old men and women were also not spared. Dholki pulled them along. All came to know alphabets and a bit of writing. They learnt how to do things and a bit of craft too. They were surprised and happy to make and use things of their own making.

Now they could understand the language of the kids and vice versa. Communication was not such a big hurdle anymore.

The jungle people knew many herbs, roots, fruits and flowers and the medicines made from that. Even the sight of some blind children was restored with some of those juices and herbal cures. They could see better. From the juice of some leaves, they got a balm made that enabled some of the lame children to walk better. They continued to stay there for quite a long time.

They got the hint of mines of coal and petroleum in that Green Island. They came to know about the existence of many more precious ores and minerals in the island. Flags were planted there as landmarks for future use too. There were many useful plants like rubber in the island. But the three pioneers were far from being fully educated themselves. They had got to this island from their adventure of a picnic in the forest and all their learnings were already used up. Had they studied more they would be using these things still more and in a better way. Paltu said, "Had I been a scientist, I would have harnessed the minerals and forest resources so much better and made the people happy."

Oltu said, "Had I been an engineer I would have made so many buildings and plants here. In the absence of roads and bridges, we have not been able to go to many places and they have continued to stay uncivilized.

Dholki said, "Had I been a doctor, then nobody would suffer so much in diseases in this island. I would be making useful medicines from the plants of this island." Now all of them felt how precious study and education was. Earlier they were so vexed with the advice of their parents and so annoyed with the continuous lessons by teachers. So even when exams were near, they had come away to do a picnic. Today they were realizing the value of education in life. So many resources and wealth of the island was lying before them. But in the absence of more education, they were unable to make use of that and only living somehow from hand to mouth. All three were now pining for studies, but what could be done!

More children were coming to the forest school now. The jungle children wanted to read a lot. But how much could these teachers teach? But the forest people wanted to know more, learn more. They wanted to go ahead. They said, "We want to fly in the aero-plane and move in submarines. We want to irrigate our lands and do more agriculture, produce more crops. We shall read more, work more and live happily." It was a big problem now. The limitations of the three little Maestros would come out now. It would be known that their learning would not take one far. So, what should they do now?

Paltu always thought himself to be too clever. He said, "Let us tell them that all lessons are over for them. Studies of the world are over. And they shall get the certificates now."

Oltu was angry, "That cleverness shall not work here. Study is not to be bound up in certificates and hung on the wall. We say, 'We have read so much, learnt so much. Government does not give us a job, what shall we do? We are without a job. And Govt. is responsible for us. We shall work if we find a job.' But these forest people are hardworking and sincere. They don't want just the certificate and the stamp of education. They want to use the knowledge. They want to use the resources of this island. Studies make us more idle and make us proud. But here after study, they like to work more. They are applying it more. Agriculture, cottage industry, health and hygiene, cleanliness, in all these, and they are advancing like never before. There is no place for idlers here. So, we must somehow convince them that our own education too has not come to an end. Study in life is never finished. There is no end to it."

Student Movement in Green Island

One day Oltu, Paltu, Dholki and teacher Mohan found that none had come to the school. What was the matter? Why were the children who had such a craze to study absent?

Then they heard a noise. They came out and saw the students were moving in a long line and shouting slogans. The slogans were- 'Teach us more', 'Teach us new lessons', 'We shall grow up well', 'We shall walk shoulder to shoulder with the people of the world.'

The three kids were taken aback. Who had instigated these simple children to do this? The purpose of their agitation was noble. But by strike they could not fulfill their wishes and achieve their objectives. How could they get more lessons, new lessons, if they did not come to school and roam around on the road shouting slogans? How could they grow up well? It was the time to study for them. If they agitated now and wasted time, the unrest might subside, but where would they get back the lost time?

Wherefrom they had got this idea then? They saw in front of all, Bahadur was walking like a student leader. Then some boys and girls of their own group were following him. Now things became clear. Their own children from the den were the masterminds. They had seen the student strikes in their own country. In their country, students would not go to school for months, even if they don't know the purpose of a strike as they are prevailed upon by others. They would not study. They would indulge in arson, burning of buses, houses and the like. They did not understand that they were wasting the precious time of their own study life. Whose is the country?

Whose is the property? It is all ours. These things Oltu and Paltu were not realizing when their parents were telling them earlier. But that day they began realizing this, now that the law and order, progress and development of this Green Island was upon them.

But they were happy now that when in their country, the students used to give slogans like 'Waive the Exams', 'Promote without Exams', here the students were giving slogans like 'Teach us more', 'Teach us New Lessons' etc.

Paltu said, "Brother, let us close the school sine die to avert this strike."

Oltu said like a seasoned leader, "The afraid act like that. If you are in fear, fear shall trouble you more. All indiscipline and trouble are because of lack of understanding between teachers and students, between students and the government. We shall face them and explain things to them. If explained, even animals understand, humans certainly will."

Mohan said, "Shoot them and injure one or two. Even now in the broken ship and launch guns filled with bullets are there. For last few days the differently abled students have been demanding for more facilities and advanced methods of education. They are the root cause of this strike."

Dholki came out, "Mohan bhai, this is not expected of you. Even animals are not to be disciplined by bullet. How can you talk so about humans? Human life is so valuable. When we cannot give life, we should not think of taking life. Leave everything to me. I shall take control now."

Listening to the dear and nervous Dholki, the two brothers and Mohan were taken aback.

The procession reached the school. Bahadur was leading it. And barking his support in full blare. Oltu and Paltu were thinking, "Our students are simple and stupid like this Bahadur. They don't understand the meaning of movement. Somebody else puts them in the front to serve his own purpose. But the brunt is borne by the people at the front. Now if shoot we must, this stupid Bahadur shall be the first target. And Bahadur has no guilt. He has strength, he has enthusiasm. So, he is kept ahead. He has no reluctance to do work. How can he know what is good and what is bad? That is the responsibility of the elders, of the parents and teachers."

Dholki stood in front of all. Smilingly she welcomed all. All shouted, "We shall read new lessons. We shall form a new society."

Dholki said, "Your demand is genuine. It shall surely be fulfilled."

"When shall it be fulfilled?", asked the students.

"That is in your hands", calmly replied Dholki.

"How?", asked the students.

Dholki told them calmly, "How can you read new lessons if you roam on the roads instead of sitting in the school? You shall forget the old lessons. The more you read them, new lessons shall emerge."

Some students said, "We don't know about that. We need new lessons, subjects. We need new schools. We shall damage and destroy this old school."

Dholki asked them, "Who had made this school? With the sweat of brow, taking pains to make this out of earth and clay?"

"We", they said in one voice.

"Then your own works you are going to damage. If you damage this, you only must make another school. Whose is the loss? Yours or ours? We are the guests of your island. We are here today. We shall go back tomorrow. It is your island for you to make or break. We can't prevent you. But if you do it, you are damaging your own country and land."

The students were silent. The new does not come up by breaking the old. The old is accepted and the new is made from that.

Dholki told them again, "New ideas are within you. If you put your knowledge into use, you shall find new things. You shall make this land new. Whom are you striking against? The responsibility of building this land anew is yours. Has anyone prospered by neglecting in duty? Who has put this idea in your minds?"

Now all were looking at each other. Such a small girl! How nicely she explained it all to them? Oltu and Paltu were also surprised. This Dholki herself was not going to school and was eager to join a strike few days back. Now she was talking so cleverly when the responsibility was on her. One develops it when one is in charge.

Dholki called the guardians. Everything was explained to them.

Guardians decided that the children shall be meted out a punishment for having resorted to a strike. They said, "There was no capital punishment in the island, there is no physical punishment or inflicting of pain either. There is such a punishment there wherein the person having committed a wrong thing shall cry and repent. It was decided that punishment shall be meted to all."

One student told, "But we are demanding to be taught new lessons. Is that a fault that we should be punished?"

Paltu was angry, "Unless you come to school, how can you learn new lessons? Do you think we don't know new lessons? What do you think of us?"

Someone replied, "You are teaching us the very same lessons over and over again."

Paltu got angry now, "Listen to new lessons..."

Then he started,

"Hadu Singh, Phadu Singh- Hichang, Hichang

Kapidang, Kapidang... Khichang... Khichang

Handu Raas, Fandu Raas, Fichang, Fichang

Hling, Sling, Mling, Kling, Ghling...

Olam, Bilam!!"

All were taken aback. They had not read these new lessons.

Unnecessarily they wasted a day. The three Maestros were real adepts! The simple jungle children were won over. Dholki had controlled her laughter with a lot of effort. She had seen enough of Paltu's all-knowing style. He would suddenly do things like this. He would not think what would happen afterwards.

Anyway, the children came to school. Situation became stable. But a punishment was decided to be given to all. There was a cry-fruit in that island. If a bit of it was taken, eyes would be full of tears. Saliva would come to the mouth and one started repenting. This cry fruit was given to the guilty often there.

A big basket of cry-fruits was brought. It was to be given as per age. First was the turn of

Bahadur because he was in the lead. The fruit was beautiful like the laughter fruit, red and luscious. If one looked at it, one would salivate. Bahadur was all agog. He was hungry too. He could hardly resist. He snapped at it and took four or five. Then where would the poor fellow go? He was crying, barking and rolling on the ground. Tears, saliva and mucus all were flowing together. The mouth was burning, and he was in pain. His greed served him right. All were worried for him and caressed him. They brought cold water from the fountain and made him drink. Some sweet fruit was given to him.

Dholki patted his head, "Now, do you understand? It is better to think well before acting. It is not good to be at the forefront in everything, not in things which are not good."

Bahadur was listening to her words, twinkling his eyes and nodding his head.

New Study and New Work

Children came and sat quietly in the classroom. Paltu began to think. How to carry on now? He somehow hoodwinked them with his abracadabra for some time. But those were not real lessons. He had to confide in his brother. He asked, "What shall we do now?"

Oltu said, "It is fine. Now let us teach them

through vocation or work. Children shall do some work and earn something. But remember, we need to study a lot. We cannot appease somehow and suppress the urge for study in the minds of these children. Now we must try to get back home. We shall read a lot, be trained and then be back to this Green Island. We shall build a new and civilized society here. There shall be only one caste, creed and country and no fear of war in that society. All shall work for peace and unity."

Paltu was very happy to listen to his brother. He never knew his brother was so intelligent.

Then they started Vocational Education. Mohan himself knew a lot. Oltu and Paltu too had quite a few ideas. Clay modelling and making useful items from that was one area. Making things from moulded iron was another. Wood, coir, broomstick, banana stem and coconut branches were used to make useful things. Adults applied their intelligence. Small cottage industries sprung up.

There was no dearth of flowers, fruits, tree and plants, stones and iron etc., in the island. There was spread of agriculture, small industries and education by the children, as if it was a new town. It was like a paradise for the children now.

But civilization had gone on way ahead. Man has landed on moon. Computers are doing so much. Shall the students remain satisfied with this much? Now the three kids felt like coming home soon. They understood that by going away from home without completing studies was a real problem. They realized the significance of studies. So, they had to go back and finish their studies. But how would they return? No ship comes to this island for its disrepute as an island of cannibals. Some accidental survivors from the shipwrecks caused by the magnetic hill must have spread the news in other lands. So, no ship ever came that way.

Oltu and Paltu foisted a red flag on the Magnetic Hill. It's meaning-Danger. Don't come this way-. On the other side of the island, they flew a green flag. That meant there was no danger there. Even then no ship was coming that way. Then they told Bahadur to bark if he saw a ship standing on the hills. Bahadur barked at the top of his voice and his throat became sore. Even then, no ship came ashore. The children were keen to go back home and study a lot. Their hope to go back to the lap of the mother and motherland remained unfulfilled. They were pale and did not feel like eating. The jungle people could hardly know the pain in their hearts. There was no dearth of food, clothes and houses in the Green Island. And these children were accepted like Kings there. Everyone was as if at their beck and call. They were to rule as kings. And later their next generation should also enjoy there. What was the reason for them to be so keen to get back to their country again?

Patriotism in Children

One day all the guardians of the village asked the children as to why they were so sad. Oltu said- "Mother and Motherland are superior to heaven. Those who forget the motherland in their greed for happiness, wealth and power are like animals. For an animal every place is same if he is well-fed. But the patriotism and love for the nation and country makes a human being great and worthy. Many noble men in our country have sacrificed their life and happiness for the motherland. Those who are living and serving in other countries, are fine and right in so far as the entire world is our home and they are working for the people there and that country. But just as taking care of one's mother is our primary duty, similarly, taking care of the motherland and serving her is the sacred duty of the children of a nation."

Paltu got up and spoke, "Brothers, we shall not forget you. We shall have higher education and return to you. We shall take you up further in the ladder of education and civilization. You shall improve the lot of your own country. We don't aspire for any power. There are no rulers or subjects in our country. All are equal there. The rule is in the hands of the people. We are all citizens. We three are from the womb of the same mother. I am brown, my brother is black, my sister is flat nosed, but fair. Similarly, from this earth mother, black, brown, white, short, tall, flat-faced, curly-haired, straight-haired, blondes and brunettes, all have come. All are equal and all have a right to live here. The gods in our country are Jagannath, Balabhadra and Subhadra. Black, white and yellow. The Lord looks upon all humans of the world with the same love and compassion. He does not discriminate about caste and creed. Neither do you. You don't have any difference between the ruler and the ruled. You are like our brothers. You shall come to our country. We shall come to yours. We shall serve each other. But should we forget our own mother and motherland?"

Now Dholki stood up. She started in her dulcet voice, "Brothers! If we keep a parrot of the forest in a golden cage, and feed it very well, it shall still pine for its own mother. The golden cage is nothing compared to the green foliage of her free mother in the forest. Our condition is like that. We get lot of amenity and dignity here. But we pine for the lap of our mother. Our mother's hand is waving at us. The motherland is calling us. If you visit our country, you shall also like it there but shall be eager and keen to come back. As you have never left your motherland, you are not able to understand our missing the mother and motherland."

Dholki was driven to tears while speaking. Oltu and Paltu were also moved. Tears were shed from the closed eyes of the blind children.

Dholki sang a patriotic song, sobbing as she sang. All joined the chorus. The forest land rang and reverberated with the chanting of the glory of India. The people of the forests acclaimed, "Kudos to you, children of India. Kudos to your patriotism and humanism."

Bahadur becomes Mad

Bahadur got away to the forest in the morning. He used to jump around from hill to hill. Sometimes he ate, and sometimes he did not. He used to come back in the evening weary and exhausted. Someday he limped, and some other day had a bleeding nose. He lied down limpid and silent in the night. None could understand. What had happened to the poor dog!

Dholki pleaded with him, "Bahadur, don't jump around like this, my dear! Someday you may lose your life falling from a hill. Who told you to do so?"

Bahadur paid no heed. As if he was into some guerilla training.

Paltu said, "He shall be a leader in a circus party, it seems. So, he is practicing being a leader.

The jungle people said, "Maybe he is possessed. Or maybe someone has cast a spell of black magic on him." He was talked of like this. One day, Paltu made him eat four sleep-fruits. For four days he sat around and dozed. He badly needed rest. Else he might die. Then all said, "Let him eat a sleep fruit everyday till he is normal. At least he would get some rest."

Bahadur was very clever. Once the effect of the sleep-fruit was over, he chased Paltu to bite him. All became afraid. They thought he had gone mad.

Oltu said, "He has taken a pledge."

Dholki said, "He barked so much standing on the summit of the hill to get back to his motherland. None heeded him. Maybe in that grief, he has resolved to commit suicide by jumping from the cliff."

Oltu was annoyed, "Our Bahadur is not such a coward that he shall commit suicide. He is doing some preparation. Leave him alone."

Bahadur continued with his strange practice. He was becoming wounded and weak sometimes. Dholki used to take care of him and feed him eggs, milk and cheese etc.

The people of the jungle were sad. They thought, "No ship was coming here as we were eating human flesh. How barbaric we were! Two animals may fight each other. And one eats the flesh of another. What is the point in such a fight between a man and a man. They should be friends. But can the men in faraway ships now understand that? They think we are all brutes here."

Days passed. Now Bahadur was quite an adept in jumping from a hill to another. He almost flew in the air with confidence. People watched him like watching a feat in circus. He was called Windy Bahadur.

One day the secret of Bahadur's madness was revealed. Bahadur snatched the pen from Oltu's hands and holding it between his front legs gave the signal to him to write a letter. He would jump to a ship from the hilltop and through them send a communication to their country. Everyone was taken aback. What a patriotism of the dog!

Oltu wrote a letter. He wrote that there was nothing to fear. There was a new civilization in this island, and they could come. The letter was kept in a packet inside the mouth of the dog. Bahadur took leave from all. He might live if fortune favoured him. Otherwise, he would die while jumping on to the ship. Dholki was in tears. But she put a garland on his neck with smile on her lips. She put a red dot of victory on his white forehead. She wished him well and honoured him with a lamp light moving around his head. As if he was her son and was going to the fighting field for the country. All had good wishes for Bahadur. All accompanied him to the foothills singing patriotic songs. Bahadur happily ascended on the summit. A flag of a ship far away was already in sight.

Sacrifice of Bahadur

The ship was slowly moving towards the island. The green flag was fluttering on the summit of the hill. All were wishing the ship to know the significance of the green flag and come near. If it happened, poor Bahadur would not have to make a risky jump to reach them and deliver the message by endangering his life. Children were waving green branches. The ship was nearing. He waited for it to come ashore or at least come within the range of hearing. Then things could be told to them aloud. But alas, the ship was changing direction. Now the ship would be moving away. Bahadur did not delay. He jumped and moved like a white kite in the azure sky towards the ship. Slogans were shouted by all- "Bravo Bahadur", "Hail Mother India", "Hail Green Island", "Hail the amity of India with Green Island", "Hail Human Unity", "We are all brothers" and the like. Bahadur should surely land on the ship. He had practiced for long falling from air without harming himself. He was now nearing the ship. Now, just a little! A little more!

Hail Bahadur!

Alas, just then he fell. But what was this! He fell a little away from the ship. Just like a white ball he fell, into white foams of the waves of the sea. His face appeared, small and beautiful, in the waves of the sea and then went out of sight. An animal sacrificed his life for the sake of humans and their society.

In Memory of Bahadur, the Martyr

There was a wave of sorrow that swept across the Green Island.

A big meeting of mourning for Bahadur was arranged. Dholki was almost speechless, with tears flowing down her cheeks. Tears of all, old and young, fell like a river which would fall into the sea and reach Bahadur. All were steeped in sorrow.

Dholki controlled herself with difficulty and narrated the life story of Bahadur. Just because they had shared some food with the orphan puppy, he repaid them so handsomely standing beside them through thick and thin and finally gave up his life for them. Her voice was trembling, and she sat down.

Oltu told in a grave tone, "Bahadur is not a mere animal. He is our teacher. He has taught us patriotism, loyalty, love for humans and sacrifice of life for a noble cause. Let us not grieve for him. His soul must be blessed by the Divine. He is immortal now. There may be a divine purpose in his life. We shall resolve to work for peace and amity within the human society, thinking of him. That shall be the true tribute to Bahadur." All resolved to do the same.

A statue of Bahadur was carved in stone. It was a fine statue made by the people of the jungle. The statue was installed in front of the school. The statue of the three monkeys of Gandhiji was already there. Oltu and Paltu had already hung many pictures of leaders like Gandhiji and Netaji inside the school. Bahadur's statue was placed in the garden. The children offered flowers to him every day and went to classrooms. Dholki caressed the statue every day to express her love for Bahadur. Oltu and Paltu also stood there for few minutes remembering Bahadur.

To the people of the Green Island, Bahadur was almost a divine entity. They adored him.

All started working with enthusiasm, with new hope and fervour. The wish to return home became a vow. The ship was being repaired. The people of Green Island too joined in supporting them.

Nothing is impossible if unity and collaboration is there. The broken ship became a new one. Oltu and Paltu even took two rounds in the sea with the mended ship. Some more things were to be done. Food, drinks and other provisions had to be carried with them. There were a few leakages where water was seeping in sometimes. Those were to be sealed with the gum of the rubber tree. The renovated ship was named 'Bahadur'.

A few meritorious students of the Green Island were also eager to go to India for higher education. Some of the seniors were also keen to go to India to sign a treaty of friendship. All were thinking if something untoward happened to the ship midway, then all would become martyrs like Bahadur for the love of country and humanity.

Rebirth of Bahadur

Bahadur fell in the sea just a little distance away from the ship. There was a sound of music as he fell. Dholki had bound her anklets on his four feet. The sound claimed the attention of the sailors. They saw that a dog was about to drown in the waters. They lifted him on board. It was a surprise to see a handsome dog.

They knew he was alive as he fell a little away from the ship. Had he hit the ship he might have been dead or seriously injured for good. Bahadur was unconscious, not dead. So, his treatment started. He regained his consciousness. He was tossing his head about. The people on board were surprised. Wherefrom came such a lovely dog with trinkets, vermilion, garlands and all! Bahadur had kept his mouth closed. When he came to senses, he twinkled his eyes and took a good look around him. He could know he had succeeded! He got up and had a round of dance with joy. He had seen Dholki's Odishi dance steps and could imitate the steps and the rhythm well. He bowed and greeted all at the end of his dance. The people there were so pleased to see him and his lovely dance.

Then, Bahadur took out the letter from his mouth and showed to them. They came to know why he had kept the mouth shut. "What loyalty and intelligence of a dog!", They wondered.

They were astonished to read the letter. The Island of Man-eaters is the Green Island and a friendly country! A few urchins had made possible what was deemed dangerously impossible by the adults. There too there were special children like blind, deaf and dumb and few with walking difficulty. They had helped in the development of education and health as well! If these special children were given proper education and opportunity, they could do everything so beautifully! ▪

The Ship Comes to the Island

One day a big ship was sighted near the shore of the Green Island. The children thought that the sailors might have thought this island to have a port seeing the renovated ship anchored on the shore. They were happy now. Maybe they could return now to their country in this ship. Alas, dear Bahadur could have waited a bit longer for this day.

There was a new wave of enthusiasm in the island. After such a long time, people from friendly territory had come there. They had to be welcomed with pomp and ceremony. The people of the Green Island wore their finest clothes. They had flowers and garlands in hand. They were giving slogans of friendship.

When the ship came ashore, Lo! it was Bahadur who jumped out of it! Many of the garlands landed on his neck which was almost bent. Then came the turn of other guests. Three boys of the island sat in the pose of the three monkeys of Gandhiji. It was an indication that they were not in the mode of violence anymore. They were not for speaking, seeing or hearing evil in the world.

The captain of the ship was mighty happy and shook hands with islanders. Green Island was now a friend of theirs.

All were delighted that Bahadur was alive. They lifted him up and took him on a round of the island. Flowers were showered on him.

Bahadur saw his beautiful statue near the school and thought that another dog in his absence was doing great duty in the island. He jumped down, embraced the statue and complimented it. Seeing the naivete of otherwise intelligent Bahadur all began laughing. The captain of the ship, however, said, "It is no laughing matter. Rather we have to learn a lot from him. We humans are so jealous. We can't easily accept anyone in our place and think others to be rival to us. But Bahadur, even though an animal, has accepted another in his place and complimented him so well."

Till then, Oltu, Paltu and Dholki had not come to the forefront. The welcome celebration was on and the islanders were into it. The newcomers were quite moved by the level of joy and acceptance there. Oltu, Paltu and Dholki came out and saluted the captain.

He asked with a ring of surprise in his tone, "Are you those three truant siblings, Oltu, Paltu and Dholki?"

Oltu said gently, "Yes, Sir! But how did you know about us?"

The captain took out a newspaper. It had the picture of all three of them. Their details with appearance were described. The informers were requested to contact the parents. Their father and mother had made an intimate appeal, "Dear ones, our boys, our girl, apple of our eye! Our dear Oltu, Paltu and Dholki! Please come back. You are not bad at all, not disobedient, why did you leave the house? Without you, our sorrow knows no bounds…"

This had been appearing in the newspaper since they left home, so that they should be easily recognizable and could be traced. The three kids cried thinking of their parents. The captain said, "You might have caused sorrow to your parents, but you have ushered in a civilization in a newly discovered island and created new friends. So, they shall forgive you."

The three kids said now, "Whatsoever good work one may do, one should not disobey the parents and go away from home without the permission of parents. We had played truant to go to the picnic. We are alive today because of our Bahadur's help and our strength of mind. Henceforth, we shall take parents into confidence. They shall never stand in the way of any good work. Mahatma Gandhi had been into stealing and had confessed before his father. One should not hide anything from one's parents. They are our first teachers. If we err, they may punish us, forgive us and take us to their lap. Alas, how much pain they would have got pining for us. Please take us back to them as early as possible."

The captain patted them on the back and told, "You shall surely grow up one day to be very good and great persons. Those who love their parents, elders, and the motherland, shall surely attain name and fame. Don't worry anymore. I am cabling wireless messages to be conveyed to your parents about your achievements and your return. Your parents can watch your journey back in the ship on the television screen. We have such arrangements in place in our ship."

Oltu said, "It is not only we, but many children snatched away from their parents by dacoits are also about to return to their parents."

Goodbye to the Green Island

At last came the day of departure. The eyes of the erstwhile cannibal inhabitants of the Green Island were full of tears.

As if Oltu, Paltu, Dholki, Bahadur and all the special children there were not people from an alien land! As if they were their kith and kin, their family. But they had to return to their own country. Lots of gifts were given to them. Beautiful flowers, strange laughter and crying fruits and magnets were given to them. Oltu, Paltu and Dholki took leave from all, saluted and said, "We shall return after we become great scientists, engineers and doctors. Your children shall also come back highly educated and accomplished. They shall make this Green Island a golden land. You are our friends and are always welcome to our country. We shall also come to you. We shall cooperate in the progress of your country. You shall also collaborate with us. An evolved human civilization in this world is not possible without peace, amity, love and cooperation. Your island is so beautiful, you are all so hale and hearty because you don't fell the trees. You worship the trees. Trees are true friends of ours. Remember our request not to cut trees in future when your civilization advances. Even if you must fell a tree sometime, you should plant ten trees in its place. This should be your mantra."

The ship set sail on the blue sea. The green flag on the Green Island was flying high. All were wishing, "Goodbye, our dear little friends. Our best wishes for your prosperity, always."

The enticing and winsome view of their

parents and motherland were dancing in the mind's eye of Oltu, Paltu and Dholki.

Far away from there, innumerable children of the country were sitting glued to the TV sets at home watching them sailing back home in the ship and were proclaiming, "Kudos to the Three Maestros!"

Dr. Pratibha Ray

Author's Bio:

Dr. Pratibha Ray is a luminary in Indian literature, whose voice resonates through the pages of her Odia novels and stories, reflecting the rich cultural ethos of Odisha. She has made significant contributions to literature, earning prestigious accolades such as the Jnanpith Award, Moortidevi Award and the Padma Bhushan. Her writing often explores themes of humanism and social reform, drawing inspiration from her deep-rooted beliefs in Vaishnavism. Ray has made significant contributions to children's literature, enriching young minds with her engaging storytelling and moral lessons. Her works not only entertain but also instill values of empathy and courage, encouraging children to explore their identities and the world around them. She says, "He who does not like flowers and children is less of a human being." She lives in Bhubaneshwar, the capital of Odisha.

Website: htpp://pratibharay.com

Sankar Narayan Mallick

Translator's Bio:

Shri Sankar Narayan Mallick has worked as a development banker in the field of agriculture and rural development in various parts of India. He has worked, inter alia, as the Principal, National Bank Staff College and Director, Bankers' Institute of Rural Development and superannuated as a Chief General Manager in NABARD from Lucknow. He is a bilingual writer and poet, writing in English and Odia. He is also a translator and editor of books in English, Odia, Hindi, Bengali, and Assamese. He lives in Bhubaneswar, the capital of Odisha.

BLACK EAGLE BOOKS

www.blackeaglebooks.org
info@blackeaglebooks.org

Black Eagle Books, an independent publisher, was founded as
a nonprofit organization in April, 2019. It is our mission to
connect and engage the Indian diaspora and the world at large
with the best of works of world literature published on a
collaborative platform, with special emphasis on
foregrounding Contemporary Classics and New Writing.

www.ingramcontent.com/pod-product-compliance
Lightning Source LLC
Chambersburg PA
CBHW050418110726
47899CB00008B/2768